This book belongs to:

_____

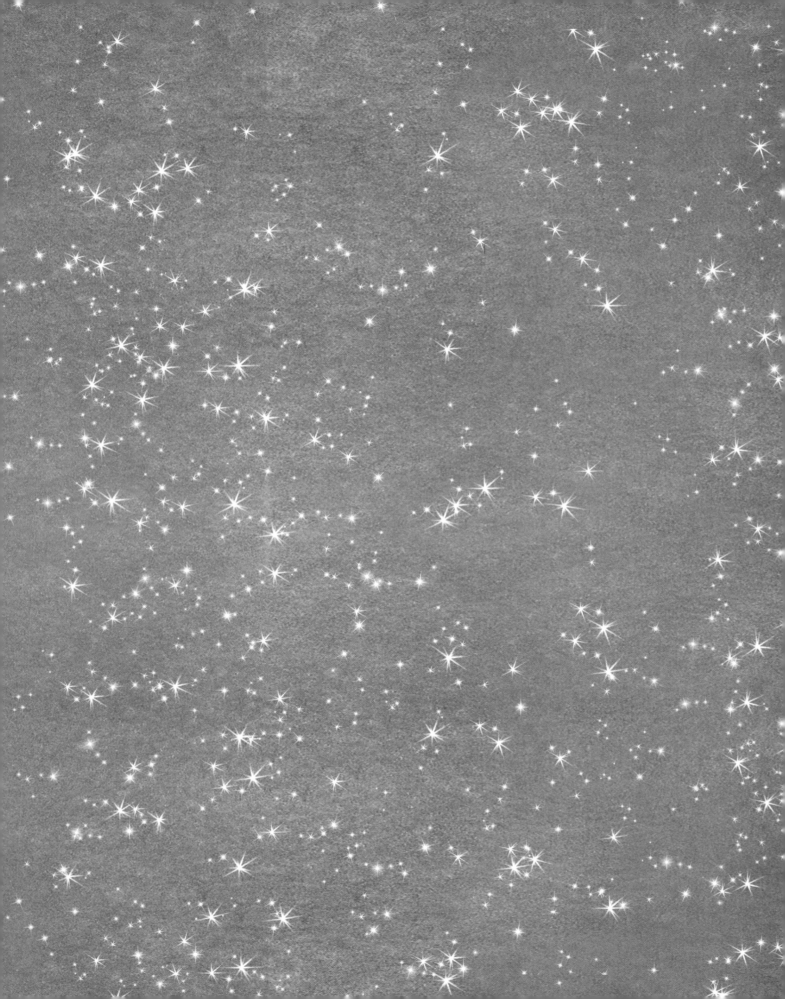

God's Little Angel™

Gabby's Stick-to-It Day

A Story About Never Giving Up

By Sheila Walsh
Illustrated by Natasha Kuricheva

A Division of Thomas Nelson Publishers

NASHVILLE   DALLAS   MEXICO CITY   RIO DE JANEIRO

GABBY'S STICK-TO-IT DAY

© 2012 by Sheila Walsh

Illustrations by Natasha Kuricheva

Published in Nashville, Tennessee, by Tommy Nelson®. Tommy Nelson is a registered trademark of Thomas Nelson, Inc.

Published in association with the literary agency of Alive Communications, Inc., 7680 Goddard Street, Suite 200, Colorado Springs, CO 80920. www.alivecommunications.com

Thomas Nelson, Inc., titles may be purchased in bulk for educational, business, fund-raising, or sales promotional use. For information, please e-mail SpecialMarkets@ThomasNelson.com.

Unless otherwise noted, Scripture quotations are from the Holy Bible, New Living Translation. © 1996. Used by permission of Tyndale House Publishers, Inc., Wheaton, Illinois 60189. All rights reserved.

Scriptures marked ICB are from the International Children's Bible®. © 1986, 1988, 1999 by Thomas Nelson, Inc. All rights reserved.

ISBN 978-1-4003-1805-6

Library of Congress Cataloging-in-Publication Data

Walsh, Sheila, 1956-
    Gabby's stick-to-it day : a story about never giving up / by Sheila Walsh ; illustrations by Natasha Kuricheva.
       p. cm.
    Summary: Sophie is a little girl who tries to be helpful but has trouble sticking to a task until Gabby, her guardian angel-in-training, finds a way to teach her not to give up.
    ISBN 978-1-4003-1805-6 (hardcover)
    [1. Guardian angels--Fiction. 2. Angels--Fiction. 3. Determination (Personality trait)--Fiction. 4. Helpfulness--Fiction.] I. Kuricheva, Natasha, ill. II. Title.
    PZ7.W16894Gbs 2012
    [E]--dc23
                                                                                            2011027711

Printed in China

12 13 14 15 16 RRD 5 4 3 2 1

Mfr: R. R. Donnelley / Shenzhen, China / January 2012 / PPO 126977

A Letter to Parents

When I became a mother, the greatest desire of my heart was to teach my son that God loves him and watches over him all the days of his life. This lesson became particularly important on that terrifying day when I dropped my son off at kindergarten for the first time. I realized that the circle of his life was getting wider and that I was going to have to depend on God to care for him when I couldn't.

One of the things that brought tremendous comfort to me was realizing that God has placed angels in charge of our children. I began a study on angels because I wanted to know what's really true and what we've just picked up from our culture. In Matthew's gospel, we read that some of the disciples had said to Jesus, "Who is greatest in the kingdom?" Christ brought a little child to Himself and answered, "Don't think these little children are worth nothing. I tell you that they have angels in heaven who are always with my Father in heaven" (18:10 ICB). That verse brought me such comfort to know that God has sent angels to watch over our children.

Through these fictional stories of Gabby, God's Little Angel™, I hope to teach our little ones that they are always in God's care. Each book in the series will focus on one of the biblical roles of angels: to protect, to guard, to encourage. God's commitment to watch over our children is so much greater than any parent could ever offer. He has sent His angels for this important responsibility. They do the will of our Father in heaven and always point the attention back to Him. That's the job of Gabby, God's Little Angel™.

Sheila Walsh

It was a glorious day in heaven, the only kind of day God's little angels know. Raffles, a senior angel, was asking Gabby and her friends about the child each angel was watching over.

"Well, sir," Gabby began,

"I love watching over Sophie.

I mean, I love her . . . I really love her, but . . . I think we have a problem!"

Matthew 18:10

"It's not that she's a naughty girl, no, no . . . far from it,"

Gabby said. "It's just that . . . Look! She's doing it again!"

"Doing what?" her friend Raoul asked, peering through a hole in a cloud.

"She's been trying to be helpful, but **she's about to quit halfway through a task.** That's three times this week, and three times is, like, a lot. I mean, it is a whole one time more than two times . . . or two times more than one time. . . . Oh, what am I going to do?"

"What else did Sophie give up on?"

Raffles asked.

"You are not going to believe this, but . . . well, I know you are going to believe it even though it is almost unbelievable," answered Gabby. "Well, she asked her daddy if she could help him paint the fence. And then she got tired and set the paint can on top of the gate and left. The can wobbled and wobbled and almost fell over onto her daddy's head, but **I caught it just in time!**"

"That would have been messy,"

Raffles agreed.

"I know!" said the little angel. "Green hair! **He would have had GREEN hair!** After that—"

"Gabby, your next assignment," Raffles interrupted, "is to help Sophie understand why it's important not to give up."

"I'm on it!" Gabby said.

"Sprinkles, get back in this tub right now!" Sophie said.

Sprinkles jumped back in the soapy water, splashing water all over Gabby, who had flown down to help.

"Now stay . . . stay, good girl," Sophie said. "I'm using Mom's very best shampoo on you, so do . . . not . . . move!"

Sprinkles jumped again and shook water everywhere.

"Sprinkles, stop it! You're going to knock over the—"

"Watch out!" warned Gabby.

She swooped down just as Sprinkles turned the tub upside down.

"That is it. I give up!" sighed a very wet Sophie.

Sophie's mom peeked out. "What's all the noise?" she asked.

"It's Sprinkles, Mom. She . . . she nearly drowned me!" Sophie said. "I was trying to help you by giving her a bath, but **it's just too hard.**"

"Well, we can't leave Sprinkles looking like a large soapy marshmallow, now can we?" her mom said. "Why don't I finish bathing Sprinkles, and you come inside and watch Ian for a bit? You could read him a story while he eats his lunch. That would be a big help."

"Okay, Mom. I will totally do that!" Sophie said.

Sophie ran inside, where her baby brother, Ian, had just begun eating. Gabby followed and waited for the story.

"All right, Ian," Sophie began. "I am going to read you a story about a caterpillar who turns into a butterfly."

"Oooh, I love this one,"

Gabby said, flying around to where she could see the pictures.

"Once upon a time," Sophie began.

Suddenly, Ian tossed his spaghetti noodles in Sophie's direction. **Gabby grabbed them just in time.**

"Ian, I can't read to you if you throw food at me," Sophie said. She began to read louder,

"Once upon a time there lived a little . . . "

Ian picked up another spoonful of noodles and threw it at
Sophie, this time hitting her right on the nose. Ian laughed and
clapped. Gabby tried not to giggle, but **Sophie *did* look silly.**

"Mom, I can't get Ian to listen to me," Sophie yelled out of the window. "He is throwing food at me and laughing, and it's—it's just ridiculously ridiculous!

I am done!"

Ian started to cry.

"Oh dear! It's okay, little one," Gabby whispered to Ian.

Sophie's mom gave Sprinkles one last rub
with a towel and walked back inside.

"So are you giving up on this job too?"

she asked Sophie.

"I know I should stick to it, Mom, but I . . . I . . . I've tried,
and it's just not working."

Gabby knew it was time to remind Sophie about some very important words from God. She sat right beside her, whispering in Sophie's ear,

"So let's not get tired of doing what is good. At just the right time we will reap a harvest of blessing if we don't give up . . . If we don't give up, never give up . . ."

Galatians 6:9

"Sophie, are you all right?"

her mom asked.

"Yes, Mom, I . . . somehow **I was just thinking about a Bible verse** I learned last week," she said.

"Which verse?" asked her mom as she took Ian out of his high chair.

"It was about not giving up . . . even when you really want to and are being attacked by spaghetti noodles," Sophie answered.

Her mom smiled. "Sounds like a good way to live. So are you going to watch over Ian while I clean up?"

"Sure, Mom. **And this time I'll stick to it,**" Sophie said.

Gabby began doing cartwheels and high-fived Sprinkles.

She planted a big invisible kiss on Sophie's head.

"**Yuck, bugs!**" Sophie said as she swatted her hair.

Gabby laughed, knowing that Sophie could not see her and thought the angel kiss was a bug.

"Wait until I tell Raoul about that one," Gabby said. "He'll get a big kick out of it. He'll laugh for **days . . . weeks . . . eons!**"

Sophie sat down with Ian, opened the book once again, and tried using her

happiest big-sister voice.

"Once upon a time . . . ," she read.

Ian looked at his big sister and gave
her the biggest, drooliest grin he had
ever grinned. When the story was over,
Sophie said in a loud voice,

"The end!"

Ian clapped, and **this time
Gabby happily did too.**

That night, Gabby was back in heaven, watching the stars with her friends Raoul and Parker.

"So, did Sophie quit again today, Gabby?" Raoul asked.

"Well, she did and then she did again and then she didn't, if you know what I mean," Gabby said.

"Nope, not a clue," Raoul answered with a smile.

"Well, she did quit, but then I reminded her of a Bible promise she had heard," Gabby said. "It was cool, so cool.

God's words changed her."

"You did a super job encouraging Sophie to stick to it when she's up to something good."

Parker said.

"I love helping her do the right thing, even if she starts and stops and starts and stops and finally starts and FINISHES!" Gabby replied.

"Well," Raoul said, "I have a big job to finish too. So . . . want to help me, old buddy, old friend?"

"Sure!" Gabby said. **"All wings on deck!"**

We must not become tired of doing good. We will receive our harvest of eternal life at the right time. We must not give up!

–Galatians 6:9 ICB